THE OLD MAN

Thanks to Bruno — Sarah and Claude

This edition first published in 2018 by Gecko Press
PO Box 9335, Wellington 6141, New Zealand
info@geckopress.com

English-language edition © Gecko Press Ltd 2018
Translation © Daniel Hahn 2018

Original title: *Bonhomme*
Text by Sarah V. and illustrations by Claude K. Dubois
© 2017, l'école des loisirs, Paris

Distribution
United States and Canada: Lerner Publishing Group, lernerbooks.com
United Kingdom: Bounce Sales and Marketing, bouncemarketing.co.uk
Australia: Scholastic Australia, scholastic.com.au
New Zealand: Upstart Distribution, upstartpress.co.nz

Edited by Penelope Todd
Typesetting by Vida & Luke Kelly
Printed in China by Everbest Printing Co Ltd, an accredited ISO 14001 & FSC certified printer

ISBN: 978-1-776571-91-8

For more curiously good books, visit geckopress.com

THE OLD MAN

By Sarah V.
Illustrated by Claude K. Dubois

Translated by Daniel Hahn

GECKO PRESS

The sun is rising over the town.
Wake up, everyone! It's time to go to school.

It's time for the old man to get up, too.

His blanket is soaked. It's been a cold night.
The old man is freezing. He'd love a cup of coffee.

If he walks a bit, that should warm him up.

He's hungry...

Really hungry.

Hey, it's Dumpling! Dumpling's hungry, too.

The old man is so tired...
It was a hard night.

He might stretch out for a bit.
Just for a few minutes.

Watch the people going by.

There's the man with the mail.

The old man remembers.
He used to deliver the mail, too, a long time ago.
Bills and love letters.

And that big dog at the house on the corner…
He can still hear it barking!

"Come on, pal, up you get. You can't stay there."

The old man's not welcome here.

He's on his way.

If only he could warm up, but the stores are closed.
It's still too early.

He'll find something to eat at the shelter.

He can hear his belly gurgling.

His turn at last.

"Your name, please."
His name? He doesn't remember… Easier to leave.

The sky darkens. It looks like rain.

There's the bus! And it's almost empty. He can warm up there
for a few minutes without bothering anyone.

He's not so cold with his feet against the radiator.
The houses roll past.

The old man falls asleep.

"Maaama! That man stinks!"
He wakes with a start.

The bus is filling up. All these people...

He feels everyone's eyes on him.
He blushes beneath his beard.

He has to get out. Quick!

The bus stops.

He feels so lonely.

Some kids are playing on the swings in the park.
Others are feeding the ducks.

A couple are kissing on a bench.

The old man is thirsty. Apart from the sparrows, he's the only one who knows how delicious this fountain water is!

There's nobody watching. The old man takes off his shoes.
Ahhh, that's better!

What if he just stays here for a bit?
No one can see him under his blanket... No one?

"Want some?"

"Do you want my sandwich?
You're funny, you look like a teddy bear!"

The little girl smiles.

It's the best sandwich in the whole world.

That evening, the old man goes back to the shelter.
This time, he has a smile inside.

"Your name, please?"

"Teddy!"

APR 1 1 2018